Fee-Fee's Holiday

Illustrated by
Andrew McLean

Meet the mice who live in Squeak Street

Old Bun lives in Number One.
His piles of gold shine like the sun.

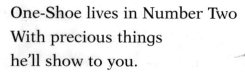

One-Shoe lives in Number Two
With precious things
he'll show to you.

Fee-Fee lives in Number Three
With her enormous family.

Pink-Paw lives in Number Four.
She paints until her paws are sore.

Fat Clive cooks in Number Five.
He makes us glad to be alive.

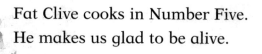

Published by
Happy Cat Books
An imprint of Catnip Publishing Ltd
14 Greville Street
London EC1N 8SB

First published in Australia 2005 by Working Title Press,
33 Balham Avenue, Kingswood, SA 5062

This edition first published 2007
1 3 5 7 9 10 8 6 4 2

Text copyright © Emily Rodda, 2005
Illustrations copyright © Andrew McLean, 2005
The moral rights of the author and illustrator have been asserted

A CIP catalogue record for this book is available
from the British Library

ISBN 978-1-905117-53-6

Printed in Poland

www.catnippublishing.co.uk

Quick-Sticks lives in Number Six.
Her band is called the Squeaky Chicks.

Kevin lives in Number Seven.
He thinks old cars
are simply heaven.

Tails the Great, in Number Eight,
Spooks us into an awful state.

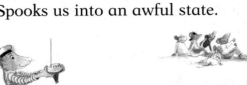

Adeline, in Number Nine,
Builds boats — all to her own d

And post-mouse Ben, in Number T
Is resting his poor feet again.

Contents

~

Chapter 1
~
Fee-Fee's Problem

Fee-Fee was a very busy mouse who had many, many children.

Her husband, Charlie, was a sailor. He spent most of his time at sea. So Fee-Fee had to care for her family all alone.

She did her very best. Three times a day, she made the children line up. Then she ticked their names off on a list, to make sure that no one was missing.

"Muffy, Fluffy, Buffy, Scruffy, Tilly, Milly, Billy, Lily, Nibbles, Tibbles, Gus, Fuss, and Naomi."

The only one Fee-Fee didn't have to count was the baby, Sweetie-Pie. She carried him around with her, so she always knew where he was.

When she wasn't counting her children, Fee-Fee worked very hard.

She cooked and cleaned. She scrubbed and washed. She never seemed to rest.

"You need a holiday, Fee-Fee," her friends in Squeak Street often said.

Fee-Fee agreed. She felt quite worn out. Her secret dream was to be all alone on a desert island for one whole week.

One night at dinner, Fee-Fee was so tired that she fell asleep with her head in her scrambled cheese.

"Poor Mama," said Tilly. "Let's do something nice to help her."

"Yes!" said Milly. "Let's make a cake!"

Everyone helped to make the cake. It took a long time. When at last the pan was in the oven, the kitchen did not look the same as it had before.

It looked very, very messy.

Fuss looked very messy too. He'd fallen into the mixing bowl. He looked in the mirror and began to wail.

Fee-Fee woke up. She saw the mess and screamed. She saw Fuss, and screamed even louder.

While Fee-Fee was running a bath for Fuss, Tilly and Milly tried to sweep the floor.

They were not very good at sweeping. Soon the mess was even worse.

"Stop that!" shouted Muffy.

She grabbed the broom, swung around, and slipped.

The broom flew out of her hand. One end smashed the teapot. The other end hit Buffy in the nose.

Buffy crashed into Fluffy.
Fluffy fell head first into the last
of the eggs.

And suddenly everyone was
fighting.

While Fee-Fee was stopping the fight, the bath overflowed.

While she was mopping up the bath water, the cake burned.

There was a lot of smoke, and the fire engine came.

Three fire fighters rushed in with hoses, and fell over on the slippery floor.

Fee-Fee pulled off her apron and stamped on it. Then she shouted: "I NEED A HOLIDAY!"

Chapter 2

~

The Competition

After the fire engine had gone, Fee-Fee sent all the children to bed. Then she put on her apron and began cleaning up.

She mopped the floor and washed the walls. She wiped the table and the stove. She put everything back where it belonged.

The children lay on their beds, listening.

"Mama needs a holiday," said Muffy.

"Let's buy her one, then," said Buffy.

They all tipped out their treasure boxes into one big pile.

Between them they had three crumbs of cheese, a red leaf, a bread crust, some silver paper, two grass seeds, a raisin and a dead worm.

"How much do holidays cost?" asked Gus in a small voice.

"A lot more than this," said Muffy.

Just then, Fee-Fee was wrapping up rubbish in some old pages of the *Mouseville News*. Suddenly she saw the word HOLIDAY.

She scraped away the tea leaves, the eggshells and the burnt cake. What she read made her heart pound.

CHEESEY

CHEWS

DO YOU NEED
A LUXURY HOLIDAY???
CHOOSE CHEESEY CHEWS
AND WIN!!!

Collect 50 CHEESEY CHEWS box labels.
In 20 words or less, tell us
what YOUR FAMILY thinks
of the GREAT CHEESEY TASTE of
CHEESEY CHEWS.

Fee-Fee squealed. The children came running, and when they saw the notice, they cheered.

But by this time Fee-Fee had read the small print at the bottom.

"The competition closes in ten days!" she cried. "Can we eat fifty boxes of Cheesey Chews by then?"

"Yes!" the children yelled. They were all very good eaters.

So Fee-Fee took off her apron and found her purse. Then they all rushed to the All-Night Munchie Market.

They came home loaded with Cheesey Chews. All their friends in Squeak Street came out to look.

Soon everyone knew about the plan to win a holiday for Fee-Fee. And everyone promised to help.

Next morning, all the Squeak Street mice had Cheesey Chews for breakfast. After the first mouthful, they all did the same thing.

They put down their spoons and said, "Yuk!"

Cheesey Chews were very chewy. They were a nice bright yellow. But they tasted nothing like cheese.

"They taste like plastic," said Milly.

"They taste like sand," said Billy.

"I don't know *what* they taste like," said Fee-Fee. "But I've never eaten anything worse!"

Pink-Paw, the artist who lived next door, agreed with Milly.

Kevin, in Number Seven, agreed with Billy.

And all the other Squeak Street mice agreed with Fee-Fee. None of them had ever eaten anything worse.

But no one gave up. Every day, every mouse in Squeak Street ate Cheesey Chews for breakfast. And Fee-Fee and her children ate them for every single meal.

Chapter 3

~

Cheesey Chews

At the end of nine long days, Fee-Fee had fifty Cheesey Chews box labels. And the idea of eating even one more Cheesey Chew made everyone in Squeak Street sick.

Now all Fee-Fee had to do was write twenty words or less about the taste of Cheesey Chews.

It was hard to think of something good to say, without telling a lie.

"What about, 'Cheesey Chews taste better than dead worms'," said Nibbles.

"What about, 'We like Cheesey Chews better than starving to death'," said Tibbles.

Fee-Fee shook her head and wrote: "My family and I will never forget our first taste of Cheesey Chews."

Then she put the box labels and the entry form into an envelope, and they all went out to post it.

That night Fee-Fee dreamed of
golden sand and rippling water.
She dreamed of waiters bringing
her cool drinks. She dreamed of
having nothing to do but rest.

Four days later, Ben the post-mouse arrived at Number Three Squeak Street, very out of breath.

"It's a letter from the Cheesey Chews Company!" he panted in excitement.

"Muffy!" Fee-Fee squealed. "Fluffy! Buffy! Scruffy! Tilly! Milly! Billy! Lily! Nibbles! Tibbles! Gus! Fuss! And Na-o-mi!"

All the children came running. Fee-Fee's paws trembled as she opened the letter.

CHEESEY
CHEWS

Dear Fee-Fee Chatter,
Congratulations!
You have won second prize in our competition!

First prize was a luxury holiday. This was won by Mr I. M. Greedy of Dim Corner.

But in many ways, second prize is even better! Soon it will be arriving at your door.

Enjoy your dream come true!

Mr B. D. Ise
Manager
Cheesey Chews Company

Chapter 4

~

The Prize

Just then, a very large truck came rumbling into Squeak Street.

It stopped outside Fee-Fee's door with a squeal of brakes. Everyone in Squeak Street ran out to see what was happening.

The truck driver leaned out of the window.

"Did you win second prize in the Cheesey Chews competition?" he called to Fee-Fee.

Fee-Fee swallowed, and nodded.

"This is the place!" the driver yelled.

Three strong mice jumped out of the truck. They began pulling a huge box from the back.

The driver grinned at Fee-Fee in a friendly way.

"So you saved up fifty box labels!" he said. "You must really love those Cheesey Chews. I can't stand them myself."

The three strong mice heaved the huge box out onto the road. It was bigger than Fee-Fee's whole house. Then they hopped back into the truck again.

"Hooroo, then!" said the truck driver.

"Wait!" Fee-Fee squealed. "What's in this box?"

"Your prize!" shouted the driver. "Just what you always wanted. A year's supply of Cheesey Chews!"

The truck roared off down the street.

The children wailed. All the
other Squeak Street mice
groaned.

Fee-Fee didn't say a word. Fee-
Fee had fainted.

Tilly kicked the box. Millions of Cheesey Chews rattled inside it. Everyone shuddered.

"This box is evil!" Tails the Great roared, taking out his magic wand. "I will make it disappear!"

Everyone looked nervous. Tails the Great's spells quite often made things explode.

"Don't disappear the box!"
squeaked little Fuss. "Mama's
holiday is inside it!"

"No, no, young mouse," said
Old Bun gently. "Holidays don't
come in boxes!"

But Pink-Paw's eyes were sparkling. "Maybe they do!" she cried.

Quickly she explained her great idea. Everyone cheered.

They put Fee-Fee to bed. Then they pushed the box to the end of the street, and started work.

Chapter 5

~

The Idea

Fee-Fee slept for hours. When she woke up, the children were standing around her bed.

"It's time for your holiday, Mama," said Muffy. "Don't look."

"I'm dreaming," Fee-Fee told herself. So she shut her eyes and let the children lead her outside and down the street.

Suddenly the ground beneath her feet was soft. She felt herself being settled into a low chair.

"Now, Mama, look!" the children shouted.

Fee-Fee opened her eyes, and saw ...

Golden sand. Gleaming water. A small green boat. A little grass hut with a cosy bed inside. Blue sky, a smiling sun, and green trees all around.

Fee-Fee's mouth fell open.

"Happy Holiday!" shouted all the Squeak Street mice.

"It's your holiday-in-a-box!" said Gus. "Pink-Paw painted it!"

"Kevin and Quick-Sticks made the hut," said Muffy.

"Adeline made the boat," said Fluffy. "One-Shoe found the pool, and Clive and Ben helped him bring it home."

"And Tails the Great asked the fire fighters to fill it," said Scruffy. "He knows them well, because his house explodes so often."

"Old Bun gave the chair, the bed and lots of good advice," said Tilly. "And *we* — "

"*We* spread out the Cheesey Chews!" said Billy proudly. "They look just like real sand. Don't they?"

"Yes," said Fee-Fee faintly. "Oh, how can I ever thank you all?"

"Just have a good rest!" everyone called. Then they quietly crept away.

One of Old Bun's servants gave Fee-Fee a cool drink. Outside, Quick-Sticks and her band began playing soft music.

It was just like Fee-Fee's dream. Her dream come true.

For a whole week after that, Fee-Fee enjoyed her holiday-in-a-box.

She sat in the chair and read.
She wrote postcards to her friends.
She went swimming. She rowed
around in the boat. She slept.

Fat Clive from Number Five cooked tasty meals for her. And the children came to see her every day with Pink-Paw and Kevin, who were looking after them at home.

Every night, as Fee-Fee lay in her cosy bed, she looked out at her beautiful view, and smiled.

"No mouse ever had such wonderful friends and family," she said to herself.

"No mouse ever had such a wonderful holiday.

"And no mouse has ever found such a wonderful use for a year's supply of Cheesey Chews."

And, still smiling, she turned over and went to sleep.